Enid Blyton™

TOY TOWN STORIES

TUBBY BEAR AND THE DECORATING

First published in Great Britain by HarperCollins Publishers Ltd in 1997

1 3 5 7 9 10 8 6 4 2

Copyright © 1997 Enid Blyton Company Ltd. Enid Blyton's
signature mark is a Registered Trade Mark of Enid Blyton Ltd.

ISBN: 0 00 172011 2

Story by Fiona Cummings
Cover design and illustrations by County Studios
A CIP catalogue for this title is available from the British Library.
Printed and bound in Hong Kong.

Enid Blyton™

TOY TOWN STORIES

TUBBY BEAR AND THE DECORATING

Collins

An Imprint of HarperCollinsPublishers

Tubby Bear was often naughty. But this morning he was EXTRA naughty.

First Tubby Bear banged his drum all around the house.

BANG

BANG

BANG!

It gave poor Mrs Tubby such a headache.

Then Tubby Bear tore up his mother's favourite recipe. He threw all the little pieces into the air to make a snowstorm.

flutter
flutter
flutter

Then, worst of all, Tubby Bear rolled marbles all over the kitchen floor. Mrs Tubby Bear slipped on them and dropped her tea tray.

CRASH
CLATTER
CRASH!

"I've had ENOUGH for one morning!" Mrs Tubby Bear complained to Mr Tubby Bear. She wiped her hot furry brow with her apron. "When you go to decorate Noddy's house, you'll have to take Master Tubby with you!"

Tubby Bear was delighted that he was going to Noddy's house.

"Can I help you decorate?" he asked excitedly as he walked with his father along the road. "Can I dip the brushes into the paint? Can I stand on the ladder? Can I paint the ceiling?"

"No, you may do none of those things!" Mr Tubby Bear told him firmly. "You would make far too much mess. You are to sit quietly on a chair in the corner!"

Tubby Bear was very unhappy sitting on the chair at Noddy's house. He frowned as he watched Noddy and his father put up the ladder. He sniffed as he watched them take down the curtains. He wiped away a tear as he watched them open the paint tin.

It was Tubby Bear's favourite colour. Bright pink!
"I'm getting a bit bored staring at yellow all
day," Noddy explained to Mr Tubby Bear. "So I
thought we would paint all the walls a nice pink."
Mr Tubby Bear scratched his head.

"But Noddy," he growled, "you will need more than one tin of paint if you want to paint ALL the walls."

"Will I?" asked Noddy. "In that case, I had better drive my car to the paint shop to buy some more tins. Will you come with me to make sure I buy just the right number?"

Mr Tubby Bear did not know what to do. He thought he should go with Noddy to the paint shop. Noddy could get so mixed up sometimes.

But Noddy's car only held two people. That meant leaving young Tubby Bear behind!

"I don't mind," Tubby Bear said from his chair in the corner. He was a lot more cheerful now. "I don't mind being left behind. I promise to stay in my chair!"

Mr Tubby Bear stroked his chin. Could he trust Master Tubby?

It was at that moment that Mr Plod the policeman passed the open window. Noddy suddenly had an idea...

"Hello, Mr Plod!" Noddy called. "Are you on your rounds? Could you just peer in next time you pass to make sure Tubby Bear isn't doing anything he shouldn't?"

"I will indeed," said Mr Plod.

Noddy and Mr Tubby Bear felt very happy as they left the house. They were sure Tubby Bear would not do anything naughty NOW.

But as soon as Noddy's car had driven away, Tubby Bear jumped down from his chair. He made straight for the biggest paint brush and thrust it into the tin of paint.

SPLOOSH!

"I *will* help decorate," he sniggered naughtily. "I will, I will, I will! And one tin of paint is PLENTY for all the walls. As long as I just do spots!"

Tubby Bear started at the wall with the window. He painted great big spots on one side... then on the other side... and then underneath the window.

The naughty bear was really pleased with himself. He thought pink spots looked so smart!

Tubby Bear was just about to paint another wall when he heard whistling outside the window.

It was Mr Plod! Tubby Bear hurried back to his chair in the corner.

"Hello, young scamp!" Mr Plod called through the window. He could not see the wall with the pink spots. "Glad to see you are behaving yourself! I'll tell Mr Tubby Bear and Noddy when I see them."

Tubby Bear smiled as Mr Plod went on his way. The naughty bear ran back to the paint tin but – oh dear! – he ran right into the ladder and knocked it over.

CRAS H!

Oh dear! again. As Tubby Bear was jumping out of the way of the ladder, he stepped straight into the paint tin.

SQUELCH!

There was hardly any paint left. Not even enough to paint spots! Tubby Bear returned to his chair very miserable indeed. Very messy too!

This was exactly how Noddy and Mr Tubby Bear found him when they came back from the paint shop.

"Mr Plod was just telling us how good you have been, Tubby Bear..." Noddy began. Then his eyes nearly popped out of his head. "Look at my wall!" he cried. "How will we remove all those spots?"

"And look at your carpet!" Mr Tubby Bear gasped. "And look at YOU, Tubby Bear. What a terrible mess!"

After a while, though, it was decided that things were not too bad. Mr Tubby Bear said they could easily paint over the spots on the wall. Noddy said he was going to throw out the carpet anyway. It was quite old and would not go with pink walls.

That just left Tubby Bear.

"A hard scrub should sort him out," chuckled Mr Tubby Bear, grabbing hold of one of Tubby Bear's ears.

"Yes!" said Noddy as he grabbed the other ear. "A VERY LONG hard scrub!"